BERNARD MOST

Catbirds & Dogfish

HARCOURT BRACE & COMPANY

San Diego   New York   London

Printed in Singapore

Catbirds

Catbirds call to other catbirds with a song that sounds like a cat's meow.

Catbirds like to be alone but are sometimes seen in pairs. They feed on fruits and insects in woods and thickets across much of the United States and southern Canada.

Next time you hear "meow" in your backyard, take a good look. It might be a catbird!

Dogfish

Dogfish are actually some of the smallest members of the shark family. There are more than sixty kinds of dogfish.

They feed along the ocean floor, hunting prawns, crabs, and other bottom dwellers, using their sense of smell. They are very common on both coasts of the Atlantic and are harmless to humans.

Do you think dogfish could do the dog paddle?

Horseflies

Horseflies don't really look like horses. They were given their name because the females bite horses. Male horseflies feed on nectar from flowers.

Horseflies have large, bulging, brightly colored eyes and are found throughout North America. They can grow as big as 1⅛ inches long.

If a horsefly ever tries to bite you, just tell it to "Giddy-up!"

Squirrel monkeys

Squirrel monkeys are about the same size as squirrels. They leap from branch to branch in trees, travel in groups, and they even play and gather food like squirrels.

Squirrel monkeys live in the rain forests of Central and South America. They are often called the most beautiful monkeys in the world.

Wouldn't it be fun to feed peanuts to a squirrel monkey?

Rabbitfish

Rabbitfish are very unusual looking! Scientists named them rabbitfish because they have rounded, bunnylike snouts, large eyes, and small mouths with buck teeth.

Rabbitfish can be found in the deeper, cooler waters of the Atlantic Ocean and the Mediterranean Sea.

Sorry, they don't really have long ears!

Mousebirds

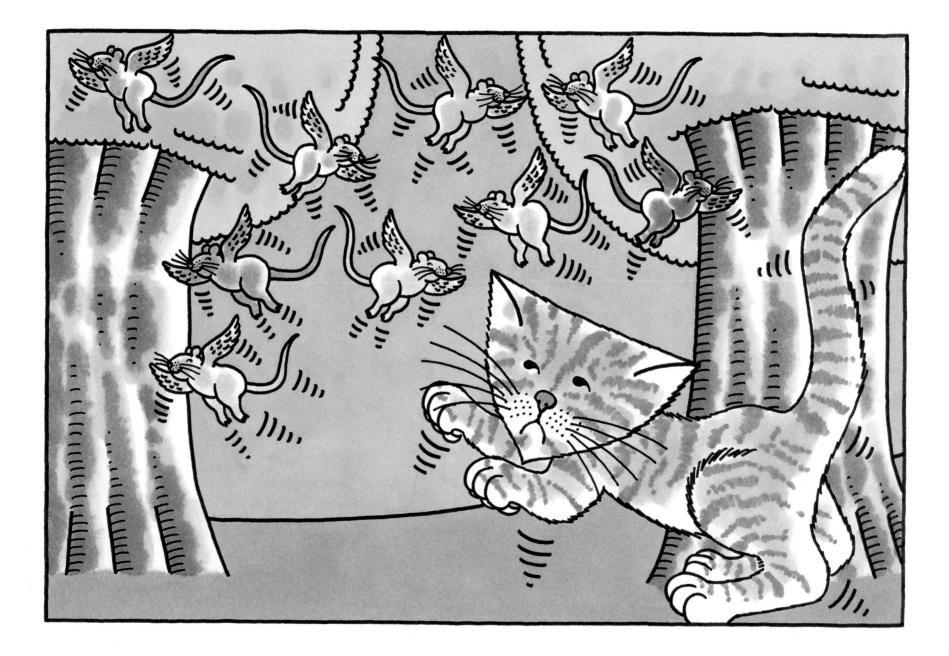

Mousebirds are small birds found in southern Africa. They creep around trees and bushes just like mice, and their feathers are a mousy color.

Mousebirds feed in groups of twenty to thirty on berries and fruits. With their short legs and strong claws, they can climb trees as well as fly.

Do you think mousebirds would be afraid of catbirds?

Spider monkeys

Spider monkeys have long legs, even longer arms, and very, very long tails. When a spider monkey swings from branch to branch, its tail acts like an extra arm or leg. Hanging by its tail, with its arms and legs free, it looks like a giant spider.

Spider monkeys can be found in Mexico and South America in groups of forty to fifty. Wouldn't it be fun to hang around with a spider monkey?

Elephant seals

Elephant seals are at least twice the size of other seals. Just one look at their elephant-like noses, and you can see how they got their name. Adult males are known for their fierce combat over female elephant seals during the mating season.

Northern elephant seals are found off the coasts of California and Mexico. Southern elephant seals are found in the Antarctic.

I think elephant seals would feel at home in the circus.

Chicken turtles

Chicken turtles don't have feathers like chickens do! But, unfortunately for them, they taste like chicken, so they are a popular food in the southern United States.

Chicken turtles are found from Virginia to Texas in the ponds, marshes, and ditches of the coastal plains. They are usually four to six inches long, although one has been found that was a record ten inches!

Antlions

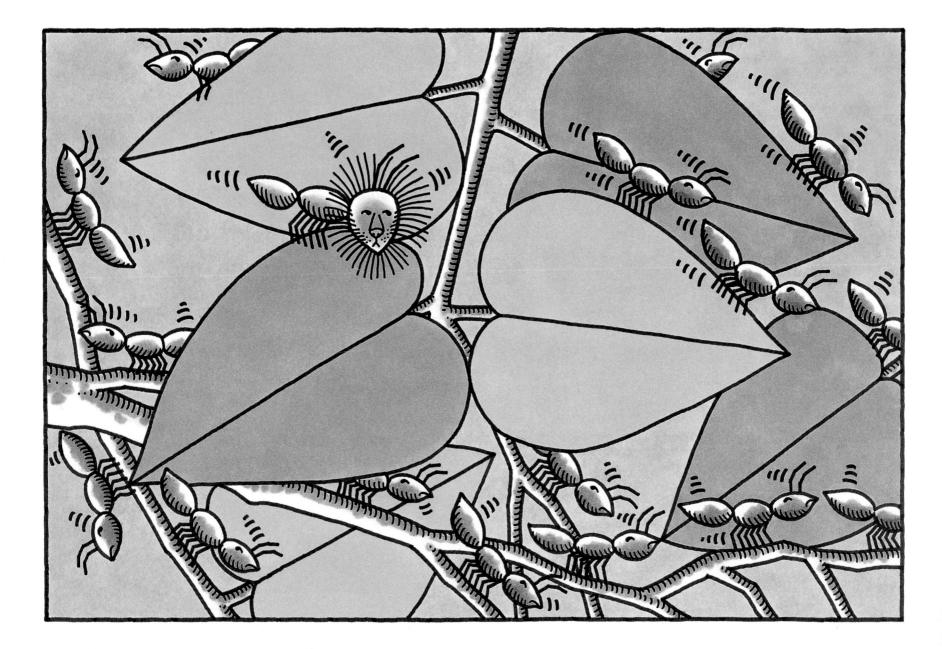

Antlions are neither ants nor lions, but they are the "lions" of the insect world.

They are known for preying on smaller insects. Antlion larvae build funnels in the sand that are like pitfalls to catch insects. The antlion waits at the bottom of the funnel for victims to fall into its sandy trap.

Like lions, antlions can be found in Africa. I wonder how many antlions it would take to roar like a lion?

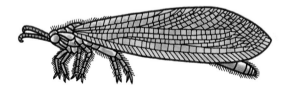

Tiger sharks

Tiger sharks are truly the tigers of the sea. One of the most dangerous sharks, a tiger shark can weigh as much as fifteen to twenty adult humans and can grow to be twenty feet long.

Tiger sharks will eat whatever they can swallow, even other sharks! Things that have been removed from tiger shark stomachs include: tin cans, boat cushions, license plates, nuts and bolts, and lumps of coal. That's why tiger sharks are also called garbage can sharks.

Pig frogs

Pig frogs don't look like pigs, but they sound like pigs! They have two different calls: a piglike grunt and a piglike snore.

Pig frogs live on the edges of lakes, bays, and marshes. You can find them on water lilies and amid floating vegetation. They are very, very shy.

They make me feel like writing a book called *The Three Little Pig Frogs.*

Dragonflies

Dragonflies are the "dinosaurs" of the insect world. Dragonfly fossils date back before the dinosaurs, to almost 400 million years ago. The fossils show that they were the largest insects ever, with wingspans of about twenty-seven inches. Maybe that's how all the myths about flying dragons started.

Dragonflies are helpful to humans because they get rid of pests. Masters of flight, they can fly backward and forward at speeds up to sixty mph!

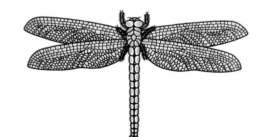

Fox snakes

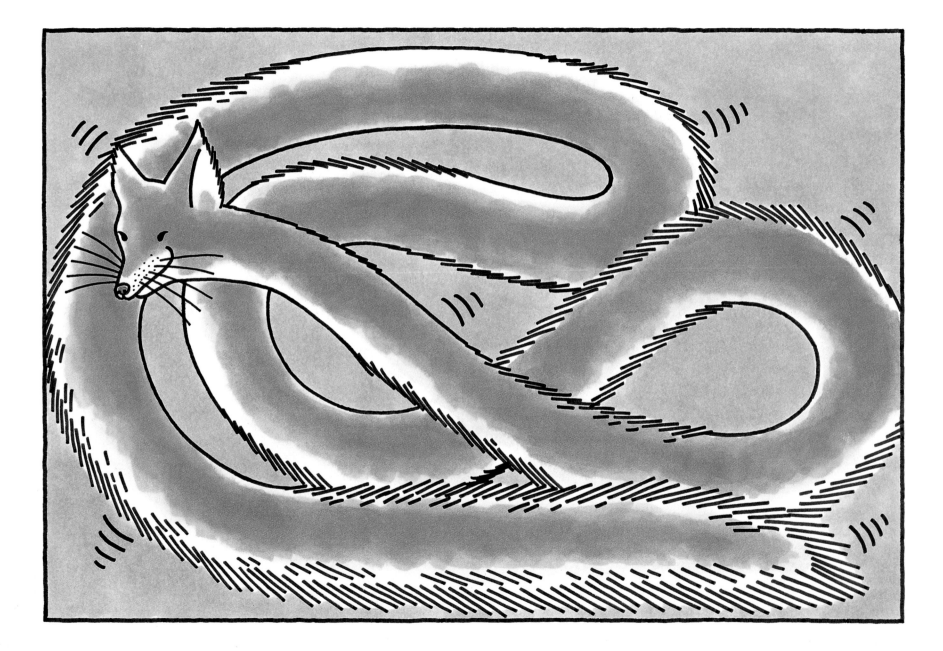

Fox snakes were given their name because they have an odor like foxes. They are also called timber snakes and pine snakes. Fox snakes grow as long as six feet, but they are harmless to humans. They feed on earthworms.

Fox snakes are found in the United States and Canada. They are good swimmers and love to sunbathe on rocks near water.

I wonder if they ever get sunburned?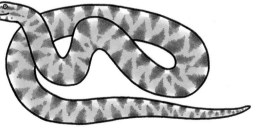

Owl monkeys

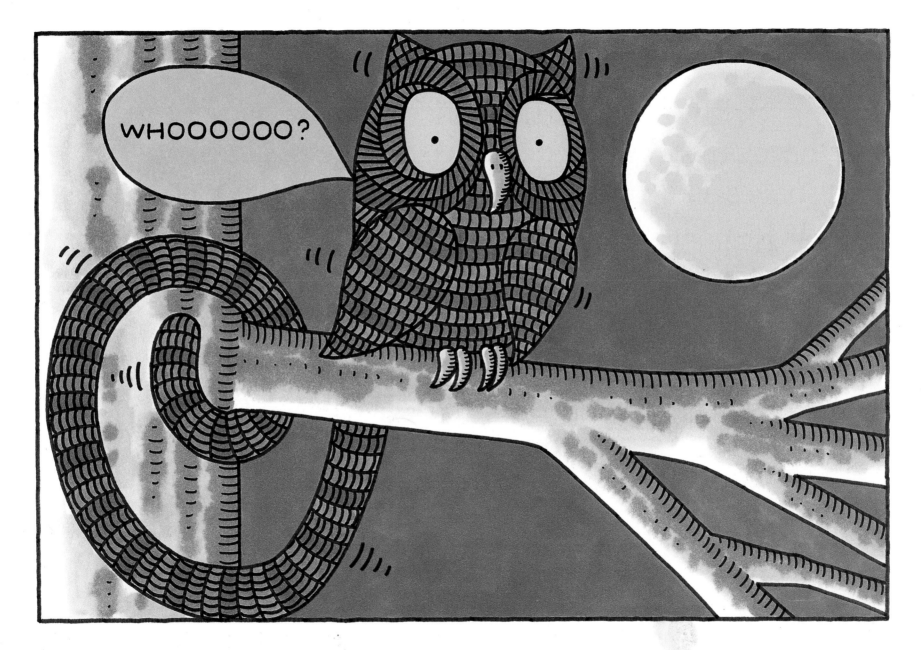

Owl monkeys are also called night monkeys. Because of their very large, owl-like eyes, they can easily see in the dark as they swing from tree to tree looking for food. Owl monkeys eat fruit, insects, and sometimes frogs or lizards. Their home is the Amazon jungle in South America.

With their short, low hoots they sound like owls, and they can be heard more than one thousand feet away.

I wonder if they are as wise as owls.

Copyright © 1995 by Bernard Most

Requests for permission to make copies of any part of the work should be mailed to: Permissions Department, Harcourt Brace & Company, 6277 Sea Harbor Drive, Orlando, Florida 32887-6777.

Library of Congress Cataloging-in-Publication Data
Most, Bernard.
Catbirds & dogfish/by Bernard Most. — 1st ed.
p.   cm.
ISBN 0-15-292844-8
ISBN 0-15-200779-2 (pbk.)
1. Animals — Miscellanea — Juvenile literature.
[1. Animals — Names. 2. Animals — Miscellanea.]
I. Title.
QL49.M83   1995
591 — dc20   94-17839

Acknowledgments:
I would like to thank my son Glenn for coming up with the title and my editor, Diane D'Andrade, for appreciating my sense of humor.

Printed in Singapore

First edition

A B C D E
A B C D E (pbk.)

The illustrations in this book were done in Pantone Tria markers on Bainbridge board 172, hot-press finish.
The display type was set in Caxton Book by the Photocomposition Center, Harcourt Brace & Company, San Diego, California.
The text type was set in Souvenir Light by Thompson Type, San Diego, California.
Color separations by Bright Arts, Ltd., Singapore
Printed and bound by Tien Wah Press, Singapore
This book was printed with soya-based inks on Leykam recycled paper, which contains more than 20 percent postconsumer waste and has a total recycled content of at least 50 percent.
Production supervision by Warren Wallerstein and Ginger Boyer
Designed by Lori J. McThomas

More books by Bernard Most:

Hippopotamus Hunt
Can You Find It?
How Big Were the Dinosaurs?
Where to Look for a Dinosaur
Happy Holidaysaurus!
Zoodles
Pets in Trumpets and Other Word-Play Riddles
A Dinosaur Named after Me
The Cow That Went OINK
The Littlest Dinosaurs
Dinosaur Cousins?
Whatever Happened to the Dinosaurs?
If the Dinosaurs Came Back
My Very Own Octopus